Contents

Ladybird books are widely available, but in case of
difficulty may be ordered by post or telephone from:

Ladybird Books – Cash Sales Department
Littlegate Road Paignton Devon TQ3 3BE
Telephone 0803 554761

A catalogue record for this book is available
from the British Library

Published by Ladybird Books Ltd Loughborough Leicestershire UK
Ladybird Books Inc Auburn Maine 04210 USA

Text © JOAN STIMSON 1994
© LADYBIRD BOOKS LTD 1994
LADYBIRD and the device of a Ladybird are trademarks of Ladybird Books Ltd
*All rights reserved. No part of this publication may be reproduced,
stored in a retrieval system, or transmitted in any form or by any
means, electronic, mechanical, photocopying, recording or otherwise,
without the prior consent of the copyright owners.*

Two Minute
Kitten
Tales

by Joan Stimson

illustrated by Tony Kenyon

The Roly Poly Kitten

Once upon a time there was a Roly Poly Kitten. He was friendly, he was cheerful and, although he didn't know it, he was just a little plump.

One day it rained so hard that the Roly Poly Kitten had to stay indoors. All morning he chased his brothers and sister.

At last lunch-time came. "Now, sit down," said Dad, "and eat nicely."

The Roly Poly Kitten bounced up to his place and tucked in. But the other kittens grumbled at him.

"Move over," cried one. "You're taking up all the room!"

"Hey!" squealed another, "you're sitting on my tail."

But, loudest of all, yelled the smallest kitten.

"Go away!" she cried. "You're a FAT KITTEN and I can't reach the food."

"WHOOOOOOSH!" The Roly Poly Kitten ran right out of the house and hid under a hedge.

"I'm fat! I'm fat!" he sniffed. "And nobody likes me." Then he took a deep breath and tried to look thinner. But that only gave him hiccups.

Back home, Dad was worried. "We shall have to make a search party," he announced.

"Ooooh, I LOVE parties," squealed the smallest kitten.

But Dad looked stern. "What I mean," he explained, "is that we must find your brother."

Eventually the kittens reached the hedge where the Roly Poly Kitten was hiding. And at the same time a stranger arrived.

"I'm looking for my son," Dad told her. "Now, let me describe him."

"Oh no!" thought the Roly Poly Kitten. He didn't want to hear how fat he was. But his family shouted so loudly that he didn't miss a word:

"He's friendly." "He's cheerful." "He's handsome." "He's strong."

"He's…" the smallest kitten thought carefully, "CUDDLY!" she squealed.

"That's right," smiled Dad. "He's a very special kitten indeed."

The Roly Poly Kitten was too surprised to speak.

"Wherever can he be?" wondered his family. And in the end they went to look at home.

Inside all was still and quiet. But not for long.

"WHOOOOOOSH!" The Roly Poly Kitten sprang out of his hiding place.

"I feel friendly," he cried. "I feel cheerful. I feel handsome. I feel strong. I feel cuddly."

"But, most of all," decided the Roly Poly Kitten, "I feel... HUNGRY!"

Another
story
tomorrow.

11

Don't Tell Tiger!

The farm kittens were planning a picnic.

"Let's eat at the old barn," they agreed, "outside if it's fine and inside if it's wet."

On the way to the barn the kittens met a cow.

"What ARE you doing?" she mooed.

"We're going on a picnic," said the first kitten. "But don't tell Tiger! He's such a ROUGH kitten."

Next the kittens met a pig.

"What ARE you doing?" he grunted.

"We're going on a picnic," replied the second kitten. "But don't tell Tiger! He's such a NOISY kitten."

Next the kittens met a sheep.

"What ARE you doing?" she bleated.

"We're going on a picnic," said the third kitten. "But don't tell Tiger! He WILL speak with his MOUTH FULL."

Next the kittens met a donkey.

"What ARE you doing?" she brayed.

"We're going on a picnic," announced the fourth kitten. "But don't tell Tiger! He tells such DREADFUL jokes."

At last the kittens reached the old barn. Tiger was nowhere in sight.

But, suddenly, "YAP, YAP, YAP, YAP!" Bully, the farm dog, appeared.

"Oh goodie," he growled, "a picnic!" And he was just about to eat it.

"What ARE you doing?" boomed a big, rough voice. It wasn't a very clear voice, because someone had his mouth full.

"Oh no!" cried Bully. "It's Tiger. He's been having a snack in the barn. And now he's going to tell me one of his DREADFUL jokes."

Bully shot off in a panic. But the kittens looked at each other and blushed. Then they looked down at their saved picnic.

"I know," they all cried together… "LET'S TELL TIGER!"

Another
story
tomorrow.

17

Catnaps

You can take one on the bus top,
You can take one in a store,
You can take one at the fun fair,
And then come back for more.

You can take one in the car wash,
You can take one if you chew,
You can take one with your teddy bear,
(I hope there's room for two!).

You can take one after playgroup,
You can take one while you grow,
You can take one when it's time to wash,
Your mum will never know.

You can take one at the dentist,
You can catnap AND still peep,
But stay awake to read these rhymes,
Then snuggle down to SLEEP!

Turn over for another kitten rhyme.

The Kitten and the Kangaroo

The kitten and the kangaroo
Were bored and wondered what to do;
"I know," said Kanga, "take a ride,
Here's my pouch, just hop inside."

The kitten took a mighty leap;
"I say," she said, "you're mighty steep;"
"Come on," said Kanga, "grab a paw,
I'll take you on a guided tour."

The twosome bounced across the town;
"Gee-up," cried Kitten, "don't slow
down;"
But Kanga groaned, "I've had enough,
I'm high on bounce and low on puff."

"But I've NO pouch," the kitten cried,
"To give my weary friend a ride;"
She thought and sighed and
thought some more;
Then rushed off to the Superstore.

The boss was kind. He heard her plan,
"I'd like to help you if I can;
Here's a trolley, take good care,
I think your friend could fit in there."

So Kanga rode back home in style;
While Kitten pushed and
gave a smile,
"I may be small, but you
will find
I'll NEVER leave a
friend behind."

Turn over for another kitten rhyme.

21

Tabitha Walker

Tabitha Walker's
A terrible talker;
She talks ALL the time;
It's time someone taught her
To go a bit slower,
Before she gets worse;
Tabitha's talking's a TERRIBLE curse!

Tabitha Walker's
A terrible talker;
She talks ALL the time;
It's time someone bought her
Some candy or carrot
To chew on instead;
Tabitha's talking's a pain in the head!

Tabitha Walker's
A terrible talker;
She talks ALL the time;
We ought to report her;
But, wait, there's a silence;
WhatEVER's the matter?
WOW! Tabitha Walker's run out of chatter!

Another
story
tomorrow.

Let Me Hear You Purr

Tom and Tess were practising their purr. They wanted to collect some money for the kitten hospital. Tom knocked on Auntie Flo's door.

"We're helping sick kittens," he explained. "And the more we purr, the more you can pay us!"

"What a lovely idea!" exclaimed Auntie Flo. "Now, let me hear you purr."

Tom and Tess took a deep breath. They began to purr their heads off. It was amazing. Somehow two purrs together sounded more like twenty!

"STOP IT!" cried Auntie Flo, all of a fluster. "You'll wake the baby. Now, here's some money for those sick kittens."

Next Tess knocked on Cousin Clive's door. "We're doing a sponsored purr," she told him.

Clive thought he was too busy to help. But then he agreed. "Okay, let me hear you purr."

Tom and Tess got started right away.

"STOP IT!" cried Clive in a panic.

"I can't hear the television. Now, here's my pocket money."

"BANG, CRASH, BANG!" Tom and Tess hammered on Grandma Gossip's door.

"Well I never, fancy that, such a kind thought," rattled Grandma Gossip. "Now, let me hear you purr."

But, as soon as Tom and Tess began, there was a frightened squawk from inside the house.

"Now you've done it – scared the parrot!" cried Grandma Gossip. "STOP THAT RACKET!"

And she tipped up her piggy bank.

By the time Tom and Tess reached home, Mum was on the telephone. At last she finished her call.

"That was Grandma Gossip," she explained, "…AND Cousin Clive AND Auntie Flo. And we've ALL come to the same decision:

"Next time you collect money for the hospital, let us hear you… *whisper*!"

Another
story
tomorrow.

29

The Kitten
Who Wanted the Sun

"What's that lovely red ball?" asked Jessica. And she pointed to the top of the hill.

"Why," laughed Mum, "that's the sun. And it's just going down for the day."

"I WANT IT!" announced Jessica, "...all for myself."

"Don't be silly," said Mum firmly. "The sun is for sharing. Without it nothing could grow and we should all FREEZE!"

That night Jessica tossed and turned. She couldn't get the bright red ball out of her mind. So, early next morning, she set off to find it.

At first the journey was fun. Jessica could see the sun quite clearly. And she purred as she padded towards it.

But then Jessica began to worry.

"However fast I go," she said, puzzled, "the sun doesn't come any nearer."

And then, to Jessica's horror, the sun disappeared completely!

Suddenly Jessica wanted to go home.

"Silly old red ball," she repeated to herself until… high in a tree, she saw it.

"Wow!" cried Jessica. "It's the sun. And I'm going to have it all to myself."

Jessica scrambled up the branches as fast as her legs could carry her. She reached forward with her paws… AND her claws.

"BANG!" There was a huge explosion and Jessica fell to the bottom of the tree. She picked herself up and ran blindly towards home.

"BANG!" There was a smaller explosion.

"THERE you are!" cried Mum. "You nearly bowled me over."

"Oh Mum," sobbed Jessica. "I've burst the sun and we're all going to FREEZE!"

Mum held Jessica close. Then she looked down at her paws. They were covered in something red and rubbery.

Mum smiled. "No kitten can reach the sun," she said. "What you burst was a lost balloon. The sun is still safe and, look, it's just coming from behind a cloud."

Suddenly Jessica felt warm and happy all over. She purred as she padded home beside Mum, watching the sun getting brighter and brighter.

Another story tomorrow.

35

Ten Go to Kitten Camp

Mrs Grey was beginning to regret it.

She had taken NINE kittens to camp and they were behaving badly.

"Now, settle down," cried Mrs Grey. "We've all had a busy day and it's time to get some sleep."

"SWISH, SWOOSH!" One of the kittens flicked his tail and tickled his neighbour. Suddenly the whole tent was flicking and giggling.

"Now really!" cried Mrs Grey.

But, just as the kittens stopped giggling…

"SWOOSH, SWISH!" Another kitten waved her tail in the moonlight.

"WHOOOO, WHOOOO!" she moaned. Strange shadows appeared on the side of the tent.

"I am the Kitten Camp Ghost," she wailed.

And very soon the tent was filled with waving tails and screams.

"Stop it at once!" cried Mrs Grey.

But, just as all was calm…

"SWISH, SWOOSH!" The kitten with the longest tail threw it across the tent like a lasso. Then she wrapped the end tightly round Mrs Grey's whiskers. And tweaked them!

"OUCH!" cried Mrs Grey. "That does it."

Nine kittens held their breath and their tails. Then they heard a terrible sound.

"SNIP, SNIP!"

Mrs Grey's scissors gleamed in the moonlight.

"You w-w-wouldn't," stuttered nine squeaky voices.

"Oh yes I would," announced Mrs Grey. And she started to cut a large piece of bandage. This was an EMERGENCY. "Look what I found in the First Aid Box!" she beamed.

Then quick as a flash, Mrs Grey fastened each kitten's tail to the inside of the tent. "NOW, settle down and get some sleep!"

"But we're not sleepy," wailed the kittens. As they swished their tails once more, Mrs Grey's emergency plan started to work – one after another, the kittens rocked themselves to sleep.

Just as everywhere went silent…

"SWISH! SWOOSH!" But this time it was only the sound of Mrs Grey's tail as SHE settled down to sleep!

Turn over for another kitten rhyme.

41

Howard's Dream

When Howard went to sleep at night,
He'd dream that he could fly,
He'd take off from his comfy bed,
And purr across the sky.

He'd wave to kittens far below,
And point up to the stars,
"Just watch me kittens, while you can,
I'm on my way to Mars!"

Now Howard knew a trick or two,
He liked to dive and spin,
And while his friends all hid their eyes,
He'd give a cheerful grin.

"There's nothing to it," Howard cried,
    "Just watch this victory roll,"
But all the kittens squealed with fright,
    As Howard... lost control.

Nine Howard lives seemed lost in one,
    As down and down he sped,
But Howard woke up just in time...
    In Howard's comfy bed.

The end.